Larry Gets Lost in the Twin Cities

Minneapolis - Saint Paul

Illustrated by John Skewes
Written by Michael Mullin and John Skewes

SASQUATCH BOOKS
SEATTLE

Thanks to all my Minnesota friends for their help: K-Rae, TJ, Eric, and Nic

Manufactured in China by C&C Offset Printing Co. Ltd. Shenzhen,
Guangdong Province, in May 2012

Published by Sasquatch Books

Book design: Mint Design
Book composition: Sarah Plein

Library of Congress Cataloging-in-Publication Data is available.

ISBN-13: 978-1-57061-754-6

www.larrygetslost.com

Sasquatch Books
1904 Third Avenue, Suite 710
Seattle, WA 98101
(206) 467-4300
www.sasquatchbooks.com
custserv@sasquatchbooks.com

This is **Larry.**   This is **Pete.**

Exploring a new city is always a treat.

A long line of cars led to a huge, crowded place.
They saw a spectacular indoor shopping space!

While his family stopped to order a bite,
Larry knew to sit still, but try as he might . . .

OF AMERICA

A growl in his stomach and a scent in the air
Led Larry to some food . . .

But then Pete *Wasn't there!*

Mall of America
One of the largest enclosed malls in the United States, the Mall of America sees more than 40 million visitors per year.

At first Larry didn't know what he should do.
He saw people going **down,** so he went down too.

On the platform below was a fast-moving train.
Maybe riding would help him see Pete again?

Pete decided on a direction
For his search to start,
But crossing a bridge
Took them even **farther apart!**

High Bridge

SAINT PAUL

Twin Cities

The Twin Cities make up the most populated area of Minnesota. It includes Minneapolis, the state's biggest city, and Saint Paul, the state capital.

1ST

Pete saw a building with
Golden horses on top.
It looked very important
And worth the quick stop.

In a park was a statue of a
Boy and his pup.
Reminded of **Larry,**
Pete vowed not to give up.

Charles M. Schulz
The creator of the world-famous *Peanuts* comic strip grew up in Saint Paul. Many large bronze sculptures of the *Peanuts* characters reside in Rice Park, Landmark Plaza, and other parks throughout the city.

FREE PARKING
MICKEY'S DINING CAR
MICKEY'S DINER

SUMMIT AVE
620 W

Pete saw many more things,
Like a fun place to eat
And some really **big** houses
All on one street.

But what he wanted to see
Was Larry's slobbering face,
So they'd have to keep looking
In some other place.

Summit Avenue
Arguably the most famous address in Saint Paul,
Summit is known for its historic mansions. Past
and present residents include F. Scott Fitzgerald,
Garrison Keillor, and the Minnesota Governor.

MINNEAPOLIS

Skyways
Downtown buildings in both Minneapolis and Saint Paul are connected by more than seven miles of Skyways so people can stay inside during the cold winters.

One building Larry passed
Was anything but square.

He also saw a nice lady
Tossing her hat in the air.

Mary Tyler Moore
A bronze statue marks the spot where she tossed her hat in the air at the beginning of *The Mary Tyler Moore Show.*

Pete didn't find Larry
By a rushing waterfall . . .

Minnehaha Falls
A popular tourist attraction
made famous by Longfellow's
poem, "The Song of Hiawatha."

And just like Pete,
Larry had no luck at all.

FOSHAY

Foshay Tower
Built in 1929, the tower
was modeled on the
Washington Monument.
It was once the tallest
building in Minneapolis.

Larry came to a riverfront that was busy and loud.
There were **bridges** and **boats**
And a **bustling crowd.**

He ran the water's edge, from end to end.
He didn't like the sad feeling of
Missing his friend.

St. Anthony Falls
The hydropower provided by the falls was used to power
the sawmills, textile mills, and flour mills that helped build
Minneapolis. The natural falls nearly collapsed in 1869 and
are now preserved and protected.

Pete and his parents kept looking,
On rented **bikes,**

While Larry took a **boat ride**
(Which is something he likes!).

Stone Arch Bridge
Built as a railroad bridge across the Mississippi River in 1883, it is now a bridge for pedestrians and bicycles.

The boat passed
Through a gate,
And then a moment later . . .

UPPER ST. ANTHONY FALLS LOCK AND DAM

The water dropped
Like **an elevator!**

Next to a structure
That was shiny and blue
Larry saw buildings
That looked not at all new.

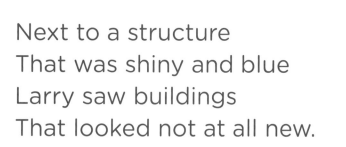

Pete was close by
Looking out from a perch,
But he didn't see Larry
Running along on his search.

Guthrie Theater
The Guthrie Theater was established in 1959 by Tyrone Guthrie as an arts center for the Twin Cities. The new, bright blue building was built in 2006 and has an observation floor and an observation deck open to the public.

Mill Ruins Park

Minneapolis was the world's largest producer of flour in the 19th century due to its location on the Mississippi River. The river provided hydropower to run the mills and a route for barges to ship the flour.

Larry crossed a **bridge**
(There are so many in this town!)
And suddenly worried that he had
Magically *shrunk down!*

He was relieved and
More than a bit surprised
To learn the cherry and spoon
Was **giant-sized!**

A boy saw Larry and asked
His dad with delight,
"Can we keep him? I'll feed him
And teach him to be polite!"

But a dog is not for taking
Just because he's alone.
The dad checked Larry's collar
And then took out his phone.

Minneapolis Sculpture Garden
Located next to Walker Art Center, the Sculpture Garden contains more than forty permanent pieces. Spoonbridge and Cherry is a 29-foot-tall water sculpture designed by Claes Oldenburg and Coosje van Bruggen.

Lake of the Isles

Lake Calhoun

Lake Harriet

Land of 10,000 Lakes
Minnesota has more than
11,842 lakes and more
peatland than any other
state except Alaska.

Common Loon
The state bird of Minnesota,
loons dive underwater to get
fish, and they let their chicks
ride on their backs.

They arrived at a big lake with many people having fun,
But Larry was interested in seeing just one.

And sure enough, **Pete was there with Mom and Dad!**
Pete hugged him and told him, "What a day I've had!"

Lake Harriet

Larry wished that he could
Share his adventure too,
But they fell **asleep,**
Because that's what
Exhausted friends do.